SCOOBY-DOO! and YOU:

A Collect the Clues Mystery

THE CASE OF THE FREAKY OIL FIEND

By Jesse Leon McCann

WORLDWIDE PUBLISHING™

SCHOLASTIC INC.

New York Toronto London Auckland Sydney
Mexico City New Delhi Hong Kong

For Truman and Louise McCann,
I couldn't have done it without you, folks!

ISBN 0-439-23156-6

12 11   7 8 9 10/0

Cover and interior illustrations by Duendes del Sur
Cover and interior design by Madalina Stefan

Printed in the U.S.A.

First Scholastic printing, February 2001

"That was scary!" you think as you walk home. You've just come from a zombie movie, and it was a good one! Lots of creepy, spooky scenes.

You pass in front of Manny's Mongolian Barbecue restaurant. Suddenly two zombies jump out of the shadows! They reach for you! *"Arrrrrrggh!!"*

You scream and jump back. Then you get a closcr look at them.

They're not zombies after all. It's Shaggy and Scooby-Doo!

"Like, you should have seen your face!" Shaggy laughs at you. "You were so spooked, you turned three shades of pale!"

"Reah! Ree-hee-hee!" Scooby chuckles.

"Thanks a lot, you guys!" you say, but you aren't mad. In fact, you start to laugh. It *was* pretty funny.

"Sorry, friend! Like, we saw you coming and couldn't resist." Shaggy pats you on the back. "Let us make it up to you. We'll buy you lunch at Manny's Mongolian Barbecue here."

The delicious smells coming from the restaurant make your mouth water. "Okay," you say eagerly.

As you enter, someone calls to you, Shaggy, and Scooby.

"Hey, guys! We're over here!" It's Fred, sitting at a table with Velma and Daphne — the other members of Mystery, Inc. "Sit down! Glad you could join us."

Shaggy and Scooby scramble over to the barbecue area against the far wall. That's where they will collect the food they want. It's all on buffet tables against the wall. The cool thing about Manny's Mongolian Bar-

becue is you get to decide *exactly* what you want to eat. You can pile up all sorts of yummy meats, vegetables, noodles, and tofu — as much as your plate can hold. Then you douse your meal with barbecue sauce and take it to the chef to cook for you.

Everything looks delicious, but you want to greet the others before getting your food. "Hey, gang! What's up?" you say as you walk over.

"We just got back from another terrific adventure," Velma says. "We spent the week in Texas."

"We solved a pretty exciting mystery. I wish you could have been there to help us," Daphne tells you. "Would you like to hear about it?"

"You bet!" you say as you sit down.

"Hey, I know!" Velma says with a smile. "We'll tell you the story of our latest case, and you can solve it!"

"That sounds like fun!" you say.

"I've even got something to help you," Fred says as he holds up a small notebook. He hands the notebook to you. "It's our Clue Keeper for *The Case of the Freaky Oil Fiend.*"

"We write down everything that happens in our Clue Keeper," Daphne explains. "The people we meet, the clues we find, and anything we think is important."

"All you have to do is read the Clue Keeper," Velma continues. "We've even added some short cuts. Whenever you see this 👁👁, you'll know you've met a suspect in the case. And whenever you see this 🔦, you've found a clue."

"Our notebook is divided into sections," Fred says. "At the end of each section, we'll help you organize the things you've found. All you'll need is your own Clue Keeper and a pen or pencil."

"Solving the mystery sounds exciting!" you say. "Let's get started."

"All right then," Velma says. "You'll see my notes on this one, since I wrote it up. Just open the notebook and begin with Clue Keeper entry number one for *The Case of the Freaky Oil Fiend*."

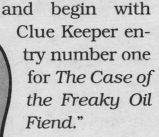

Clue Keeper Entry 1

The Mystery Machine cruised smoothly through the oil fields of Texas. We were on our way to Houston to see the Space Center.

"Like, say, Velma, is it lunchtime yet?" Shaggy asked me. "It seems like forever since breakfast, right, Scoob?"

"Reah! Rorever!" Scooby nodded, sucking in his chest so he looked skinny. *"Rook! Rime rasting raway!"*

"Wasting away?" I laughed. "Hardly, Scooby. It's only been three hours since breakfast!"

"*Zoinks!* Three hours?!" Shaggy held on to Scooby, who was pretending to faint. "Like, in dog time, that's almost a whole day! We need to get Scoob some grub right away!"

Daphne smiled and looked at a map, "Don't worry. There's supposed to be a diner up ahead by an oil refinery. We'll stop there and get you poor guys some lunch."

We drove another fifteen minutes and came to the refinery in the middle of the oil fields. A refinery is a place where they take oil from an oil well and refine it into other petroleum products. I had expected it to be full of activity. But as the Mystery Machine pulled up to the diner beside the refinery, we discovered that the diner was closed — and so was the refinery!

The only person we could see was an old guard sitting outside a security booth at the refinery gates. We got out of the Mystery Machine to talk to him.

We introduced ourselves and asked him why the refinery was deserted. "My name's Talbot O'Hare," the guard said. "I've worked at this refinery for fifty years, but I ain't seen nothin' like what's been going on here lately."

"What happened, Mr. O'Hare?" I asked.

"And, like, what do you do for food around here?" Shaggy added. Both he and Scooby rubbed their hungry bellies.

O'Hare pointed to a shed nearby, on the other side of the chain-link fence surrounding the refinery. "There's lots of grub in that storage shed," he said. "Help y'self. Ain't nobody else around to eat it."

"Like, c'mon, Scoob!" Shaggy cried happily. He and Scooby trotted inside the gates toward the storage shed and disappeared inside.

"The refinery's empty because it's haunted," O'Hare said sadly. "It began last week. The men were in the middle of their work when this creature appeared. It was some kind of fiend covered in crude oil. Or maybe it was *made* of oil!"

"Jinkies!" I said.

"The men are so scared of the Oil Fiend, they won't work here anymore. Nobody else will, either." O'Hare frowned. "But, if you ask me, the owner of the refinery and oil fields, J. D. Steerhorn, got what was coming to him."

"Why's that, Mr. O'Hare?" Fred inquired.

"Steerhorn's granddaddy tricked my granddaddy out of all this land," O'Hare said. "By all rights, this land and its oil should be mine!"

Fred, Daphne, and I looked at each other. Here was an employee with a gripe against the boss. That spells "possible suspect" in our book.

"Do you mind if we take a look around, Mr. O'Hare?" Fred asked.

"Help y'self," O'Hare said as he got up and hobbled over to an electric cart nearby. He got inside. "I was just about to take my lunch break, anyway."

With that, O'Hare drove inside the gates past the storage shed.

"I think there's more to this mystery than meets the eye," Fred said. "Come on, let's go fetch Shaggy and Scooby and get to the bottom of this."

Only, we didn't have to fetch them — they suddenly came running out of the storage shed toward us. They both looked frightened out of their wits!

"*Zoinks!* There's a greasy ghoulie in there!" Shaggy yelled. "And it's trying to get us!"

Scooby was right behind him. *"Relp! Relp!"*

We turned to look. We couldn't believe our eyes!

Out of the storage shed came a creature that looked like a blob covered from head to toe in thick, black, crude oil. And it seemed to glide, as if on a carpet of oil. It growled angrily, *"Grrrroooooowl!"* It was the Oil Fiend!

"*Jinkies!* You can get back to the exciting story after you've made an entry in your Clue Keeper. Did you see the 👁 👁 on page 8? That's your tip that you've found your first suspect. Now answer the questions below about this suspect."

1. What is the suspect's name?

2. What does he do at the refinery?

3. Why would he be glad that a monster is haunting the refinery?

Clue Keeper Entry 2

The Oil Fiend moved very fast, gliding over the ground like oil. And it was dripping tar-like drops as it reached for us.

"Hurry, gang!" Fred yelled. "Let's go up there!" He pointed to one of the tall exhaust towers where gas fumes were once burned off. It looked like a metal smokestack with a stairway spiraling upward around it.

Around and around, higher and higher we climbed. When we were about halfway up, I took a chance and looked behind us. I hadn't heard the creature growl for several seconds.

"Hey, everyone, look!" Shaggy pointed below. The creature was so oily, it couldn't climb the stairs. Instead, it kept slipping down. Finally, it growled in frustration, and slithered away smoothly, disappearing from sight.

"Whew! That's a relief!" Fred sighed. "Now maybe we can figure out this mystery."

"Well, we're not going to find any clues up here," Daphne commented. "Let's take the bridge over to that platform."

We climbed up a few feet more to a bridge that ran straight out from the exhaust tower to a platform atop a nearby tank. The tank looked like a big ball with a flat top and was colored bright yellow.

Suddenly, we heard a gruff voice. "What are you kids doing?!"

Scooby was so scared, he jumped into Shaggy's arms. *"Rooooh!"*

A chubby, short man was climbing up to the platform from the far side of the tank. He had on brown coveralls.

"We're from Mystery, Inc.," I said. "We're trying to gather clues about the Oil Fiend."

We told him about our run-in with the slick oil creature.

"*Hmmph!*" the man said. "My partner and I haven't been able to catch him so far. What makes you kids think you'll have better luck?"

"Then you've seen him, too?" I questioned.

"Sure we have. The legend of an Oil Fiend haunting the pipelines has been told here for ages," the man muttered. "My dad worked here before I did, and he heard the story, too. But this is the first time the creature has shown himself in fifty years."

"I wonder why he's back now," Fred said.

"He's back all right," the man said. "My name is Roger Culber. My partner and I once worked at this place. Now we've opened our own detective agency. We've been hired by the Steerhorn Oil Company to get to the bottom of this puzzle."

"Do you mind if we help?" Fred asked. "We've had a lot of experience solving mysteries like this."

"I think this case requires detectives who

know every inch of this refinery," Culber
scoffed, "not a bunch of kids."

Just then, a big, tall man joined us on the
platform.

"That's my partner, Hal Holt," Culber
said. "Find anything, Hal?"

Holt wiped his sweaty forehead with an
oily rag. "No, no sign of anyone except the
old guard and these kids."

Culber looked at us, "Well, we've got lots
of investigating to do. If we can't figure out
what this creature is, the workers won't be
able to come back to their jobs."

"We'll just look around anyway," Fred said. "If you don't mind."

"We do mind!" Roger Culber answered angrily. "In fact, I want all of you out of this refinery right now!"

Shaggy and Scooby's Mystery-Solving Tips

"Like, did you spot the 👀 on pages 16 and 17? Groovy! Then, get your Clue Keeper and answer the questions below about the last chapter."

1. Who were the two suspects in the last chapter?

2. What are they doing at the refinery?

3. Why do they want to solve the mystery?

Clue Keeper Entry 3

We climbed down from the big, yellow, ball-shaped tank and worked our way over to a nearby building pretending to leave. When Culber and Holt went inside, we ran back and ducked into the doorway of a nearby building. It looked like the offices for the refinery's clerical staff.

"I bet we can solve this case faster than those two can," I said.

"Me, too," Daphne agreed.

"Let's split up so we can cover more ground," Fred suggested. "Shaggy and Scooby take the offices upstairs. We'll search below. Who knows? Maybe you'll find some food up there."

At the mention of food, Scooby and Shaggy were up the stairs and out of sight.

Daphne, Fred, and I searched the first office downstairs. The lights wouldn't turn on, so we had to search in the dim light that filtered through the dusty windows.

We suddenly heard a loud *creak*, like a door opening. We almost jumped right out of our skins! Was it the Oil Fiend launching a surprise attack?

No. As we turned to the sound, we saw a man wearing a big cowboy hat stomping down the hall toward us. "Y'all must be the kids my detective Talbot told me about!" the man said. "I followed your footsteps right in here. My name's J. D. Steerhorn and this here's my refinery."

Steerhorn angrily threw his cowboy hat on the ground and started to stomp on it. "Oh! I'm madder'n a polecat caught in a clothes dryer!" he shouted.

"Don't worry, Mr. Steerhorn," I said. "We'll figure out what's going on here. I'll bet your refinery will be back open in no time!"

Steerhorn looked grateful. "Aw, thanks, kids! But that's what Holt and Culber are supposed to be do- ing. I'm old and I'd like to retire soon! But the whole town is counting on me to keep this place open. They depend on the refinery to provide them with jobs. If I can't get this place running again, the townfolk will all be angry at me."

"Why don't you just sell it?" I asked.

"This refinery is old and doesn't produce like some of the new ones," he explained. "Nobody wants to buy it. See what you kids can find out and I'll pay you."

22

"That won't be necessary, Mr. Steerhorn." Fred laughed. "But there is one thing you *can* do for us."

Fred whispered into Steerhorn's ear. Steerhorn listened for a second, then nodded his head. He and Fred shook hands. Steerhorn went out, got back inside his limousine, and sped away.

We went on searching for clues. The office had rows and rows of filing cabinets. Besides those, there wasn't much to be found. That is, until I looked down!

Fred and Daphne's

Mystery-Solving Tips

"Jeepers! Did you see the 👀 on page 21? He could be an important suspect. Open your Clue Keeper and answer the questions below."

1. Who is the new suspect?

2. What does this suspect have to do with the refinery?

3. Can you think of a reason he might want to close down his own oil refinery?

24

Clue Keeper Entry 4

"Jinkies!" I said. "Fred, Daphne, look at these!"

On the ground were two black wavy lines that ran from beside a row of filing cabinets and out the door that we'd just come in through.

"Now what do you suppose could have made those tracks?" Fred wondered thoughtfully.

I reached down and touched one of the lines with the tip of my finger. It was oil!

We only had a second to wonder what this meant, when . . .

"Fred! Daphne! Velma!"

It was Shaggy calling us from one of the offices upstairs. He sounded very excited! As quick as we could, we ran out of the office and up the stairs.

"Hurry! Scoob and I found something!" Shaggy hollered. He was *definitely* very excited.

Up on the second floor, we checked several offices before we found them. We didn't know what to expect. What had they discovered?

We found them sitting in a lunch room. They were at a table piled high with candy bars, cookies, sodas, and crackers. Both their mouths were full of goodies as they smiled and waved to us. Then Shaggy pointed to a vending machine against the wall.

"Like, lucky for us, I always carry lots of quarters!" Shaggy grinned.

"*This* is what you called us up here for? Vending machine goodies?" I asked them, folding my arms sternly.

They grinned. "It, like, was important to us," Shaggy said, shrugging sheepishly. "And we thought you'd like —"

Suddenly, we heard a terrible scream.

"*Eeeeeeeeeeee!*"

It was Daphne!

Fred, Shaggy, Scooby, and I raced out of the lunch room and onto the second story balcony that ran the length of the building. Daphne was nowhere to be seen!

"Like, what are we going to do?" Shaggy pulled at his hair, worried.

"You can start by looking down!"

Fred, Shaggy, Scooby, and I all looked over the railing. There was Daphne, hanging over the edge of the balcony.

"Little help?" she asked.

We all quickly reached over and helped pull her up.

"What happened, Daph?" Fred asked.

"I found more oil tracks up here on this floor," she explained. "I was following the oil tracks and I guess it got too slippery.

The next think I knew, I slid over this railing."

"More oil tracks?" I wondered as I looked down. Sure enough, there were the two thin, wavy lines we'd seen before. We hadn't noticed them when we ran upstairs. We decided to follow the tracks, making sure not to step on them.

We followed the trail down the first floor hall and out a back door. It kept going out onto the refinery grounds, winding

through pipes and around tanks and smoke-stacks. At one point, we came to a big, empty tunnel. We could see that the tracks led inside.

"I guess we just have to keep going," I said.

"No, we don't," Shaggy disagreed.

"Come on," I insisted, entering the tunnel along with the others.

Luckily, we always carry a spare flashlight with us. Unluckily, after we walked several hundred feet into the tunnel, the flashlight's batteries quit on us.

We were plunged into total darkness!

"Shaggy!" I scolded. "Wasn't it your turn to replace the batteries in the flashlight?"

"I told Scooby to do it," he replied.

"Roops," Scooby said meekly in the blackness.

Oops was right! Now we would have to continue on in the dark.

That was bad. Then we heard something right behind us that made things worse.

"Grrrrrroowwl!"

"I know how you feel, pal," Shaggy said to Scooby. "My stomach is growling, too."

"*Grrrrrroowwl!*"

The awful sound filled the tunnel again.

"I don't think that was Scooby," I said nervously.

Slowly, we all turned and saw a horrible sight.

"**W**rite down the clue you found in the last entry. Did you see the 🔦 on page 25? Great! Grab your Clue Keeper and answer the questions below."

1. What was the clue found in the last entry?

2. What does this clue have in common with the Oil Fiend?

3. Could any of the suspects have left the clues? Which suspects?

32

Clue Keeper Entry 5

"Run!" Daphne cried. She and Fred raced ahead.

But I slipped and fell behind. The Oil Fiend grabbed my arm. I could feel its slick fingers holding me. I squirmed but couldn't get loose.

"*Jinkies!*" I cried.

Shaggy and Scooby stopped and ran back to help me. "Like, let go of Velma, you gob of goop!" Shaggy demanded bravely. He tried to pull the creature off me, but it just pushed Shaggy aside.

Scooby bit the beast on its ankle. It immediately let go. But I guess Oil Fiends don't taste so good.

Scooby spat. *"Rastes rawful!"*

Scooby's bite gave me the chance to break loose. Up ahead, I could see light. The end of the tunnel! "Follow me!" I yelled as I ran toward the light. "Let's get out of here!"

"Like, you don't have to ask us twice!" Shaggy answered from somewhere in the darkness.

"Run! Run!" Scooby yelped.

We dashed toward the end of the tunnel. We could tell the fiend was right behind us because it kept on growling and howling!

"Hurry!" Daphne called to us. She and Fred were waiting at the end of the tunnel.

I made it to the end of the tunnel. I turned to see how Scooby and Shaggy were doing. "Jinkies!" I cried.

Some oil on the ground had caused Scooby and Shaggy to slide. They went faster and faster, bending their knees like they were surfing.

"Like, hang ten, beach doggie!" Shaggy laughed. "This is what I call riding the pipeline!"

"Reah! Ree-hee-hee!" Scooby laughed.

They didn't see that the Oil Fiend was gliding right alongside them.

The three of them slid out of the tunnel at the same time. Fred, Daphne, and I jumped back to get out of their way.

Just then, something flew off one of the creature's feet. It hit me in the head and knocked me backward into a puddle of water. My glasses went flying. Oh, great! Now I couldn't see! I fished around in the water for my glasses and found something.

I held it in front of my face. It wasn't my glasses. It was a small wheel that the Oil Fiend had lost, about two inches wide.

How strange! I searched some more and found my glasses.

Now I could see again. I looked up to see what the Oil Fiend was doing, just in time to see it limping as it retreated into the tunnel. I could have sworn it was muttering to itself! Why was it limping? How had it hurt itself?

Velma and Fred were helping Shaggy and Scooby to their feet. They were safe. For now.

"**W**ow! What a scene! The only thing worse than having a creepy creature around is to have one around when you can't see. And speaking of seeing, did you see the ⊶ on page 36? Terrific! Now, take your Clue Keeper and write down your answers to the questions below."

1. What is the clue you discovered in this entry?

2. Where did it come from?

3. What do you think its owner used it for?

Clue Keeper Entry 7

Daphne walked back to the side of the tunnel and knelt down. "This is weird," she said picking up something brown. It was a box. The side read BLACK RUBBER SCUBA DIVING OUTFIT. ⟢ We opened it up. Inside was a pair of rubber flippers and a mask. Fred reached in and took out the flippers and mask. But the black rubber suit was missing.

From the picture on the box we could tell it was the kind of scuba suit that covered a swimmer from the neck to the ankles. "And look at this," Daphne said. She lifted a roll of long black garbage bags from the box. "I wonder what this is doing with a bunch of scuba stuff," she said.

I showed the others the wheel I'd found.

"Hmmm." Fred pondered. "I'm starting to get an idea of what might be going on here. Let's follow that creature!"

"B-Back into that spooky, dark tunnel?" Shaggy stammered. "But we still don't have a flashlight! Like, that's nuts!"

"Reah, ruts!" Scooby agreed.

"Don't worry," Fred said confidently. "I have a feeling that Oil Fiend is going to be busy for a while."

Once more, we entered the dark tunnel. Once more, we were totally blind, feeling our way along. Suddenly we heard a loud noise. Then a spotlight hit us. Now we were blinded by too much light.

"Zoinks!" Shaggy cried as Scooby jumped into his arms. "Like, it's the lube job lunatic!"

Daphne and I giggled. "Don't be silly," Daphne said. "It's Mr. O'Hare, the security guard."

Sure enough, the old guard was pulling up in his electric cart.

"Hey there, young 'uns!" Mr. O'Hare said. "Need a lift?"

"Let's take it," I said. "I don't think the Oil Fiend is about to show up. I noticed that he seemed hurt. Maybe he's gone off some-where to rest. And it's too dark to find any clues."

We all gratefully piled into the electric cart. It was a tight fit, but Mr. O'Hare was able to squeeze us all in. Soon we were on the other side of the tunnel and back into the light.

"I've got a meetin' with J. D. Steerhorn," O'Hare told us. "Seems he wants to talk to me about some special deal he made with this young fellah." O'Hare pointed to Fred. "Well, see ya!"

O'Hare sped away in his electric cart. We all looked at Fred. What special deal? Fred just smiled mysteriously.

"Never mind about that right now," Fred said. "We've got to get prepared. I've got a hunch about how we should deal with this Oil Fiend."

"Like, I know the perfect way!" Shaggy suggested. "We get in the Mystery Machine and vamoose!"

Fred laughed and shook his head. "No, we go to the supply shed."

It took only a few minutes to walk there. But in that short time, I'd almost dried out in the hot Texas sun. We entered the shed cautiously. After all, this is where Shaggy and Scooby had first seen the Oil Fiend.

Fred gathered supplies: a rubber hose,

42

and batteries for our flashlight. Shag and Scoob gathered some supplies, too: cupcakes and donuts. We were so busy, we didn't see the shadowy figures until they stepped into the light.

"*Yaaaah!*" This time Shaggy jumped into my arms and Scooby jumped into Daphne's.

It was Culber and Holt, the two investigators. "Darn," Holt said, frowning. "We thought for a second we'd finally found the Oil Fiend!"

"We told you kids to leave!" Culber

shouted. "This is dangerous business and no place for kids!"

Shaggy nodded toward his cupcakes and donuts, now scattered on the floor. "We just came back for a few supplies," he said, climbing out of my arms. "We'll collect them and be on our way."

"See that you do!" Culber growled, and the two investigators left the supply shack.

"Come on," Fred said, after they'd gone. "We've got an Oil Fiend to catch!"

Shaggy and Scooby's
Mystery-Solving Tips

"Like, did you notice the far-out clue on page 39? Cool! It's a really important clue! Make sure you answer all the questions below in your Clue Keeper."

1. What was the clue you discovered in this entry?

2. What do you think this clue is used for?

3. Which of the suspects do you think uses this clue?

Clue Keeper Entry 8

" . . . and that's our plan to catch the creature!" Fred finished explaining. "Any questions?"

"Like, only one," Shaggy said. "Why is it that Scoob and I are always picked to be bait for the monsters?"

"*Reah!*" Scooby frowned.

"It's simple." Daphne smiled sweetly. "You two are the fastest runners in the group. After all, you've had *so much* practice."

Scooby suddenly looked very proud. "*Rat's rue!*"

"Like, flattery will get you nowhere!"

Shaggy countered. "Scooby and I won't do it!"

"Rat's right!" Scooby frowned again, remembering what the discussion was about. *"Rattery rill ret rou rowhere!"*

I pulled out a handful of Scooby Snacks. "I'll bet you'll do it for some of these!" I grinned.

"Zoinks! On the other hand, Scooby Snacks will get you *everywhere!"* Shaggy exclaimed.

"Reah! Reverywhere!" Scooby agreed.

Everyone got into their places. It was time to see if Fred's plan would work.

Shaggy and Scooby entered the dark tunnel once again. (After the mystery was solved they told us what happened next.) They had the flashlight, but they didn't turn it on. They remained in the pitch black.

"Like, even though we've been through here twice already," Shaggy said nervously, "it doesn't seem any *less* scary!"

"Right!" Scooby agreed as he tried to peer through the darkness.

Then, suddenly . . .

Swoosh!

They stopped short. "Like, did you hear that, Scoob, ol' pal?"

"Raybe," Scooby said, lifting one ear.

Swoosh! Swoosh!

"Y-you m-must have heard that!" Shaggy stuttered.

Scooby still wasn't sure. *"I rink ro."*

"Huuurooooowwl!"

"Zoinks! You *definitely* heard that!"

"Ripes!" Scooby yelled. *"Reah! I reard rat!"*

Shaggy banged the flashlight against the tunnel wall. It snapped on. They were grateful when the tunnel lit up brightly. That is, until they saw what was standing right in front of them!

"Hurrrrrgh!"

It was the Oil Fiend, grabbing at them with outstretched hands!

Shaggy and Scooby ducked under the monster's arms and ran in the direction of the oil field.

Swoosh! Swoosh! Swoosh! The creature followed close behind! And it wasn't limping any longer, but going *really* fast! They ran out of the tunnel and into the sunlight.

Now we could see them again as we peered out from our hiding places. The creature stayed right with them. Shaggy and Scooby jumped over a long gas pipe that lay in front of them. So did the Oil Fiend.

"Grrrrrooowwl!"

They came to a big, round storage tank. Turning to the left, they circled around it. The Oil Fiend turned right.

And they met in the middle on the other side! Now it was right in front of them!

The fiend grabbed them! It had Scooby by the tail and Shaggy by the shirt.

It was pulling them closer. It growled evilly.

"Like, good-bye, Scoob! This is it!" Shaggy hugged Scooby.

That was the cue! Fred was hiding on the other side of the pipe. He jumped up, hold-

ing the rubber hose that he'd dragged over from the nearby pump house. Back at the pump house, Daphne and I turned the hose's nozzle and the water sprayed out at full force.

Whooosh! All the water washed off the oil.

Now the Oil Fiend just looked like a man in a scuba suit wearing a mask.

We ran over to him. He was moaning dizzily.

Fred pulled off his mask.

Munch! *Munch!*

Shaggy and Scooby were finishing their second helping of Mongolian Barbecue. You've only finished your first since you've been so involved with the story, and writing down clues.

Scooby and Shaggy get up and go for *thirds.* It is, after all, "all you can eat." And they can eat a lot!

"Well, now that you've met all the suspects and found all the clues," Fred says, "do you think you can solve the mystery?"

You smile and say you think you can.

"Terrific!" Daphne says. "Here's some advice — look at your list of suspects and clues, then answer these questions."

"First, who do you think had a good reason to scare people away from the refinery?" Velma asks.

"Second, who do you think had an opportunity to dress up like the Oil Fiend?" Fred asks.

"Third, who do you think had the know-how to scare people away?" Daphne asks.

"See if you can eliminate any of the suspects first," Velma suggests. "Then, using all of the information you've collected as well as your own smarts, try to figure who the Oil Fiend really is."

"Like, I'd like to know how hot this extra-hot Mongolian barbecue sauce *really* is," Shaggy says as he dips a spoon in and tastes it. Then his face turns red and he sticks out his tongue. "Like, *yeowwwch!*"

"Really rot!" Scooby decides.

"Why don't you solve the mystery while I

get Shaggy a glass of water?" Daphne says.
"Then when you think you've got it figured
out, we'll tell you who was behind the mystery of the Freaky Oil Fiend."

You start thinking very carefully.

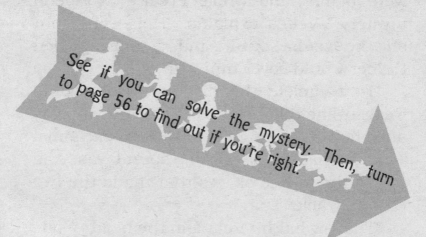

See if you can solve the mystery. Then, turn to page 56 to find out if you're right.

"**R**oger Culber and his partner Hal Holt were behind the whole Freaky Oil Fiend mystery," Velma explains. "Holt would put on the scuba outfit and a mask. Then Culber would cover him with oil."

"To complete the disguise, Holt would wear in-line roller skates to give the appearance he was gliding like oil," Fred exclaims. "That's what the *swooshing* sound was. And it was the in-line skates that made the two thin oil tracks."

"That's what hit Velma in the head — one

of the in-line skate wheels! It broke off and flew through the air. That's why he was limping," Fred continues. "When we saw the creature later, he must have repaired his skates."

"Since Holt and Culber had worked at the refinery, they knew about the Oil Fiend legend, and they knew how to get around the refinery," Daphne says. "They also knew that if they scared away all the workers, J. D. Steerhorn would hire them to solve the crime. No one else had hired them and they

wanted to get their new detective agency going with their first case. After a while, the Oil Fiend would disappear forever because Holt would stop dressing up like him. They'd claim to have chased him off and solved their first case. The town would be grateful to the two detectives for opening their refinery again."

"They thought they were almost finished — until we came along," Fred adds. "They had to make us think there was an Oil Fiend, otherwise we'd tell Mr. Steerhorn everything was fine."

"You know that our other two suspects were J. D. Steerhorn, the refinery owner, and Talbot O'Hare, the security guard," Velma adds.

"Steerhorn wanted to retire so I thought maybe he was the one. He might have created the trouble to close down the refinery without anyone in town being angry with him," Daphne comments. "But he seemed like too good a business man for that. Just shutting down the place would cost him a lot of money."

"And Mr. O'Hare couldn't have been the creature — he was too old. He had to drive around the refinery in an electric cart. No way he could have skated like that," Velma says.

"There's one thing I don't understand," you say. "What was it you whispered to Mr. Steerhorn, Fred? And why did Mr. Steerhorn want to meet with Mr. O'Hare?"

Fred smiles. "J. D. Steerhorn offered us half his fortune if we could solve the mystery of the Freaky Oil Fiend. I merely suggested that he should give half of his estate and his refinery to Talbot O'Hare."

"It's only fair," Daphne says. "After all,

Steerhorn's grandfather did swindle Mr. O'Hare's grandfather out of all that land, rich with crude oil."

"Now Mr. Steerhorn and Mr. O'Hare run the refinery and the oil field together," Velma concludes. "In fact, they make pretty good partners and they're making some great improvements at the refinery. With two people running it, it will almost be like a half retirement for both of them."

All the Mystery, Inc., gang are now looking at you.

"So, how did you do?" Daphne asks.

"I'll bet you solved the mystery like a pro!" Velma smiles. "You're pretty smart."

You smile.

"I'll tell you what *really* smarts — that hot sauce!" Shaggy winces. He holds an ice cube to his tongue. *"Thoinksh!"*

"Ree-hee-hee!" Scooby laughs and starts eating Shaggy's meal.

"Cut ith ow, Thooby-Doo!" Shaggy says as he grabs his lunch, the ice cube stuck to his tongue.

You get up to go.

"Come back and visit us again," Velma says. "There's always plenty of mysteries that need solving. Right, Scooby-Doo?"

"Rooby-rooby-roo!" Scooby cheers, in full agreement as he goes back to the barbecue for *fourths.*